Mail Order Lillian

Book 1
An Impostor for Christmas

Cheryl Wright

Copyright

Mail Order Lillian
(An Impostor for Christmas – Book One)

Copyright ©2021 by Cheryl Wright

Cover Artist: Black Widow Books

Editing: Amber Downey

Dedication

To Margaret Tanner, my very dear friend and fellow author, for her enduring encouragement and friendship.

To Alan, my husband of over forty-six years, who has been a relentless supporter of my writing and dreams for many years.

To Virginia McKevitt, cover artist and friend, who always creates the most amazing covers for my books.

To You, my wonderful readers, who encourage me to continue writing these stories. It is such a joy knowing so many of you enjoy reading my stories as much as I love writing them for you.

Table of Contents

Chapter One

Boise, Idaho – 1880's

Lillian Hanover stared out the window at the snow flurries and shuddered, then turned to study her cousin. "I have to find another job. Horace is both revolting and persistent." She pulled her shawl further up and around her shoulders. "He cornered me in the storeroom yesterday. It was all I could do not to gag."

Her cousin Joy's eyes opened wide in shock. "He… cornered you? That disgusting pig! Did you manage to get away?" Joy appeared quite concerned at her cousin's predicament.

"I did, but I have no idea how much longer I can put him off." She brushed the hair back off her face and glanced up again. "Perhaps I should do what you did and become a mail order bride. Either way, I have to get away from here." Not that Lillian wanted to go that route, but she had few options available to her.

"About that…" Joy's face suddenly fell, and Lillian wondered what could be wrong.

"Is everything all right?" Lillian asked, hurrying over to where her cousin sat. "You look quite distressed."

The two women had practically grown up together. Their fathers were brothers, and each family had lived on the same property, meaning they spent much of their time together playing. The pity of it all was their fathers were both killed in the same shocking accident on the property when a large tree fell. Five men died that day.

"I…" Joy took a deep breath, then glanced up at her cousin. "I need to ask a favor," she said far more quickly than Lillian had ever heard her speak before. "A rather big favor."

"Ask away." Now her interest was piqued.

Joy suddenly sat down and clasped her hands tightly in her lap. Her eyes were focused on her hands, rather than the person she was speaking to. Lillian felt quite concerned at this turn of events. "I am beginning to panic, dear cousin. Please tell me what ails you." Her heart pounded as she waited for her cousin to speak again.

Joy suddenly pulled a letter out of her pocket and handed it over. "I am supposed to leave tomorrow to meet my groom and marry him." Her head slowly came up until their eyes met. "I… I can't go. Will you take my place?" She let go of a deep sigh and Lillian could do nothing but stare.

"But…" She shook her head. She couldn't take her cousin's place, not when Joy had already accepted the proposal. And why didn't she want to go now, anyway? Her head suddenly felt as though it was filled with a thousand drummers, and she dropped into the chair next to her cousin. "Wha—why?"

Joy's eyes dropped to her lap again. "I've met someone, and we plan to marry." She glanced up and continued. "I had already promised to marry Simon Watson by then, but…" Tears filled her eyes. "I'm in love with Timothy Chambers, and he with me. I couldn't bear to marry someone else."

Lillian sputtered at her words. "Why would he marry me? I am not the one he's been corresponding with."

Joy suddenly stood. "Then don't tell him. Let him believe you are me."

Had she not been sitting, Lillian was certain she would have landed in a heap on the floor.

Despite the short notice, Lillian was packed and ready to leave in time to meet the stagecoach at seven the next morning. Early enough that Horace Periwinkle would not see her waiting for it to arrive. If he happened by, Lillian wasn't sure what she would do apart from ducking into the stage office for refuge.

She clung tight to the supplied ticket, along with the letters from her potential groom. The name on the ticket was Joy Hanover. She had to pretend to be her cousin. At least until she arrived at her destination. Otherwise she'd waste this Simon Watson's money. And that was the last thing she wanted to do.

Lillian had no idea what she was letting herself in for. Joy told her he was a rancher, but little more. For all she knew, he could be old enough to be her father, or even her grandfather. Heaven help her. She would devour the letters on her way to meet him and pray to the Good Lord she hadn't let herself in for anything untoward.

Her wardrobe was scarce, but she'd packed whatever she could fit. Her clothes were not fancy by any means, and depending on the situation she found herself in, may not even be suitable. She assumed she would be living on a ranch outside of the nearest town, but she couldn't be sure. Joy had divulged precious little, which was a huge concern.

The stagecoach pulled up in a rush, likely because it was running almost fifteen minutes late by the time it arrived. The last thing Lillian needed was to be spotted by Horrible Horace, as she'd come to call him privately. He was just as likely to drag her all the way to the church and force her to marry him before letting her marry someone else. He'd told her as much when he'd cornered her like a scared rabbit in the storeroom.

The thought made her shudder. She couldn't stand being in the same room as the man, let alone the same house, or heaven forbid, the same bed. "Miss Hanover?" The coach driver touched her shoulder, trying to bring Lillian back to the present. "Are you Miss Joy Hanover?" He stared at her when she didn't respond. It was then Lillian remembered she had to take on the persona of Joy.

"I, I'm sorry. I was thinking about something else." She handed over the ticket, and he checked it over, looking her up and down as though he wasn't convinced she was who she portrayed herself to be. Of course, he was correct, but Lillian couldn't tell him so. Suddenly he handed her ticket back, then opened the coach door and helped her up. Lillian sat quietly inside the coach as her luggage was loaded, still not certain she'd made the right decision. As she glanced out the window, she noticed Horrible

Horace heading to work. She slunk down in her seat, grateful she was in the middle where she wasn't so visible. No matter, her heart pounded regardless, lest he should notice her.

It wasn't until he unlocked the door and went inside the store that Lillian began to relax. When the coach took off with a thud, she let out the breath she'd been holding. She was finally on her way to her new life. A life that didn't include Horace, but included a complete stranger.

She pulled the letters out of her reticule and read every letter her cousin and soon-to-be husband had shared. That last thing she needed was to be taken unawares. If he turned out to be an ogre, according to the letters anyway, she planned to alight the coach before reaching her destination. What she would do then, she had no idea.

Lillian's eyes opened wide in astonishment as she read through the letters Joy had given her. Her head was pounding at the gravity of what she'd let herself in for. More fool her for not reading the letters the moment her cousin handed them over.

At least she now knew her groom was not old and decrepit, and she would be living on a ranch, an environment she was very comfortable with. The thought made her think about her dear parents, both of whom were no longer of this earth.. After the accident, they'd been forced to move into town. Their lodgings on the ranch were only for workers, and they'd struggled for some years after leaving. Ma cleaned to support them and had worked herself into an early grave by the time Lillian was twenty. Life had been relatively easy and happy until Pa died. It broke her heart, and that of her mother, to lose him. Truth be known, Ma had died of a broken heart. Lillian thought she might end up the same after Ma's passing, and if it wasn't for Joy, she might well have done.

As she read page after page of letters from Joy's betrothed, she understood why Joy backed out. Not because of Timothy Chambers, if he even existed, but because of these letters. It appeared her cousin had accepted Simon's hand in marriage very early in their correspondence – before Simon had disclosed his closely guarded secret.

Lillian was tempted to get off at the next stop, but knew she would be stranded with no job and no hope for the future. She really had no choice but to continue to her destination.

Chapter Two

Samson's Creek, Montana – 1880s

Simon Watson paced the sidewalk, waiting for the stagecoach to arrive. Blasted thing was never on time. Not that he had to meet it often, but on the rare occasion he did, it was always late.

He had made all the arrangements with the preacher and was ready to take the plunge. He was still rather tentative about such a huge step, but he wasn't getting any younger, and he wanted an heir. No, he *needed* an heir. The child his wife had provided was a girl – not much use to a rancher. Even if she had wanted to help, which she couldn't as she was far too young, he couldn't allow it. Women working ranches? It was unheard of. Not that he didn't love his daughter, he did. He loved her deeply, but she couldn't do the work a son could and would eventually do.

They had planned far more children, and God-willing, there would be boys amongst their brood. He sent for the doctor the moment he realized it was all going awry, but it was too late. Esther had been far too young to die, but there was nothing he could do. It was a miracle his daughter had survived, and for that, he would be eternally grateful.

It pained him to take another wife, especially after losing the love of his life in childbirth, but a man had to do what he had to do. Besides, how was he expected to raise a small child alone? Until now, his housekeeper had helped, but Martha had decided to retire, more's the pity. He couldn't blame her, he supposed. The woman was, after all, nearly fifty, and her husband had decided he wanted her home with him. She had worked for Simon for many years now, more than he cared to remember. He couldn't cope without someone to care for Ella, hence the decision to remarry.

He sighed as he stared into the distance. *Was that dust he saw?* Perhaps the stagecoach was finally arriving, and about time, too. Keeping a man waiting this long was beyond ridiculous. Particularly when he had plenty to do on the ranch.

He brushed the flurries from his suit jacket and loosened his tie – the darn thing was choking him.

The only time he wore a tie was to church, his wedding, and his wife's funeral. This time around, the marriage ceremony would be quick, but still deserved his respect. His future wife also merited his respect, and that's exactly what she would get.

He stepped back as the reckless driver pulled the stagecoach to a sudden stop. How this driver even kept his job, Simon would never know. He had driven this route for several years now, and was as irresponsible today as the day he started. As the dust settled, he moved in closer, scanning the inside of the coach for his bride. Several women sat inside, along with two older men. No photographs had been exchanged, so picking out his promised wife would be difficult.

From what he could see, only two of the women fit her description. Mid-twenties, slim of build, brown hair, and five feet four inches. Although their height was undecipherable as they continued to sit inside the coach. The two men were no gentlemen and scrambled out before allowing the women to disembark. The older of the women left the coach soon after the men, her head held high. She was vaguely familiar, and he wondered, was this woman the old schoolteacher, many years retired? Next was the blacksmith's wife, and that left only two who met the criteria.

He studied them both, his heart hammering in his chest, and he contemplated which one was his bride.

"Joy? Joy Hanover?" he said as the last of the women alighted. But neither answered. One woman clutched a handful of letters, and he wondered if this was his bride. "Joy," he said again, this time touching her shoulder, and finally her head shot up.

He felt a smile working its way across his face, but she did not reciprocate. Instead she looked startled, like a deer that had barely missed being hit by a wagon, and he wondered if his soon-to-be wife had some sort of mental deficiency, but her letters didn't indicate that. Unless someone else had written them for her.

"Simon Watson?" She finally seemed to come to her senses. "I'm sorry. I am exhausted from the long trip, and my mind was elsewhere." Now she smiled, and he breathed a huge sigh of relief. He was quite alarmed for a moment there.

"Here's Miss Hanover's luggage," the driver said, placing her scant baggage at his feet. The man was a fool, but Simon felt obliged to give him a tip, and handed over a few loose coins. The driver stared into his hand, then left them alone.

Simon leaned down and picked up her luggage. "Do you want to freshen up before we head to the church? The ladies' room is in there," he said, pointing inside the stage depot office.

Without another word, she turned and left him standing there. Simon stared after her, wondering exactly what he'd let himself in for.

She wandered out some time later, looking far better than when she went inside. Her hair, previously disheveled, had been straightened and put back into place, and her pale face now had some color. Her gown was still as creased as it was before, but that was much harder to fix. Her bonnet sat loosely on her head and had not been fastened. Simon wondered what she looked like without it. "Are you ready to be married?" He wasn't one to mince words and had no intention of starting now.

Her head shot up, and she glared at him. "We have not exchanged more than a dozen words, and you are already pushing me into marriage?"

She looked affronted, which had him puzzled. "That was the plan, if you recall." Had she decided to back out? After all this planning and working around the arrival of the stagecoach, had she changed her mind? He'd paid for her ticket, and expenses, and now…? He wasn't sure what to think.

She glanced between Simon, and the letters tightly gripped in her hands. His bride might appear better than when she arrived, but it was now obvious the trip had been far more taxing on her than he'd first imagined. "You led me to believe you needed to marry. To get away from Boise as quickly as possible."

She squeezed her eyes tightly closed. "I did," she whispered, although she had never explained the reason.

"The preacher is waiting – if you are ready. Or would you prefer refreshments first?" He stared into her face. She appeared torn as to how she should proceed. His heart thudded. What a total waste of time this had turned out to be.

She reached out and touched his arm, and a shudder went down his spine. "I'm sorry. I am totally exhausted from my long trip and can't think straight."

He could understand that. She'd traveled from Idaho to Montana, presumably with hardly a break in between. Days of sitting in a stagecoach – he wasn't certain he could endure that himself.

"It was surely grueling," he said out of the blue, then reached for her hand. His fingers closed around hers and this time, a shiver ran up his arm.

"We stopped overnight at…" She grappled for the name of the town. "Hellcat Creek?"

He couldn't help but chuckle. "Hilliers Creek, more likely. It's a small town, pleasant."

She grinned, and it warmed his heart. It was the first time she'd truly smiled since she'd arrived. His bride stared into his face, her gaze never faltering. "I'm ready to get married now." She tipped her chin up just a little. Enough for him to see she could be determined when she put her mind to it. He groaned inwardly. What on earth had he let himself into?

The wedding ceremony was over before it had barely begun, and Lillian's head was spinning. Her dreams of a beautiful wedding with her friends surrounding her had been shattered. Still, it was not her husband's doing. This had been her choice, her decision to take her cousin's place. If she hadn't fled, hadn't got away from Boise and Horace, she could be in a far worse situation right now.

Besides, Simon seemed like a decent sort of fellow. He seemed a little gruff to begin with, but she was warming to him. He wasn't difficult to look at, and that smile – it lit up his entire face. She could definitely live with that. The thing she wasn't certain about, was the one thing her cousin had omitted; Simon had a young daughter.

He had been forthcoming in his letters and had been completely open. He talked about his wife dying in childbirth, his soon-to-retire housekeeper, and the fact he must marry to keep his ranch running smoothly.

Ella needs a mother. The words were short and succinct, but they hit home. Every child needs a mother. There was no doubt about it. Lillian had already decided to disembark at Hilliers Creek for the overnight stay, but not return to continue her journey. She would simply stay in her room and decide what to do after that. Her mistake had been continuing to read the letters Simon Watson had written about his young motherless daughter. She sounded like a sweet child, but what experience did Lillian have with children? Absolutely none!

His heartfelt words had tugged at her heartstrings, and by morning she had determined to continue her journey. If not for Simon, but for the little girl who needed a constant in her life. Besides, where was Lillian to go if not to Samson's Creek? She had little money, and if she absconded with the expenses Simon had supplied, that would be… stealing. Heaven forbid she did such a thing. She was better than that, and she knew it.

No, she would not let him down.

Now that they had married, her future had been determined. There was no backing out now. Like it or not, she was a mother now, and once she arrived at that ranch, she better at least pretend to like the child. After all, it wasn't Ella's fault her mother had died, or Lillian's fault that Joy had tricked her into taking her place.

After they'd partaken light refreshments, they headed immediately for the ranch. It was a little over thirty minutes away, according to Simon. At least she wouldn't be completely isolated. The road they traveled was rough and surrounded by thick bushes. If it had been dark and she was alone, Lillian knew she would be terrified. Of course she was used to living out of town. She grew up on a ranch until her father was killed. Her heart thudded at the memory of it all, and she swallowed back the emotions threatening to seep through her eyes.

She was startled as a hand reached out and covered hers. "Everything all right? You seem a little quiet."

She turned and stared at him. "I was just thinking about my father," she said, her voice breaking. "He was killed in a ranch accident when I was a child."

He squeezed her hand and brought it to her lips. "I'm sorry. Do you want to talk about it?" She shook her head almost violently. That was the last thing she wanted to do right now. Lillian knew she would become a blubbering mess in front of her new husband, and he didn't need to see that. He would always remember her like that.

"I thought you might bring Ella with you today," she said quietly, determined to change the subject.

His eyes pierced hers as he gazed into them for a long moment. Did he see through her intentions? Today was supposed to be a happy day. Wasn't it meant to be the best day of her life? Instead of wearing a beautiful gown, she'd married in the same crumpled dress she'd worn for days. The only chance she'd had to change was during her overnight stay. There she had soaked in the bath for as long as she was able, despite the filthy state of it. When the pounding on the bathroom door began, she reluctantly got out. Lillian knew it was selfish, but she needed it, knowing what was ahead of her.

She glanced up at the archway that sat in front of her. *Rocky Ridge Ranch* – the words had been burned into the wood, and by the looks of it, had sat here for some years.

"It was originally my father's ranch – I inherited it when he died a few years ago."

"*Rocky Ridge Ranch*. Where does that come from?"

"It was originally called Samson's Creek Ranch, after the town, which was named after my father. Later on, he decided it sounded too self-centered and changed it, but it was too late to change the name of the town. My father built the town when he realized the nearest town was too far away." He chuckled then. "I don't know how he managed it, but he did." He turned to face her then. "He was a determined man, my father." He suddenly turned away, and Lillian felt his pain. It was the same pain she endured every time she let memories of her father seep into her own heart. This time, it was Lillian who covered his hand with her own. He stared down into his lap, then glanced at her. He said not a word, but something seemed to pass between them. It gave Lillian the feeling everything was going to be all right.

Except for the fact her husband believed she was someone else entirely.

Chapter Three

Simon pulled her scant luggage down from the wagon. Looking at it now, he really should have taken her to the mercantile for more clothes. Did she need other necessities, too? Joy hadn't mentioned she was in a dire situation in her letters, only that she needed to leave Boise as soon as possible. She had been quite tight-lipped about her reasons, but who was he to pry? She would tell him in her own time, if at all.

He glanced up at her as she waited for him on the porch. Standing there, he took in her beauty and her poise. Any man would be glad to have her for a wife. But she wasn't Esther. He had met her when they were teenagers – when her family had moved to town. Working the ranch with his father, he didn't get much time to himself, so the only time he saw her was at church. He later joined the youth group just to get a glimpse of the beauty who would one day become his wife. Little did they know what lay ahead.

"Boss, Missus." The voice of his foreman brought him out of his dark thoughts, and Simon glanced up. Tucker had pushed him into marrying again. *Ella needs a mother*, he'd said more than a handful of times, and Simon knew his foreman was right.

He glanced toward his wife standing, waiting on the porch. "Tucker, this is Joy, my," his words faltered, but he had to be strong. "My wife." She scowled at him, and in that moment, Simon knew she'd heard his reluctance to use her title. Her smile suddenly changed to a frown, and her face went pale. He had hurt her feelings. No, more than that, he'd upset her. He'd known it was going to be hard marrying again, but he'd had no idea how difficult it would actually be.

"Let me take that," Tucker said, taking her luggage out of Simon's vice-like grip. "You need to carry your wife across the threshold," Tucker said quietly as he grinned.

It had been some years since he'd lost Esther, and now he had to get her out of his mind. Nearly five years had passed and Ella had been motherless all that time. Thanks to Martha, she had grown into a caring and thoughtful child. If it had been left up to him, she would have turned out to be a tomboy for sure.

He climbed the few steps to where his new wife stood. He couldn't believe his luck. She was incredibly beautiful. She had an elegance about her he hadn't expected. As he came to stand beside her, he lifted her into his arms. She was a tiny thing and didn't even reach his shoulders. She squealed as he picked her up, not expecting it, then stared into his face. Her eyes scanned every line, every crevice, every part of his face. Then her hand came up, and she ran a finger along his jawline. It sent a shiver down his spine. At that moment, he wanted to kiss her and more, but Simon knew his daughter would be inside, waiting to meet her new mother.

He opened the door and carried her across the threshold, his eyes never leaving hers. He saw the longing in her face; she wanted him to kiss her as much as he wanted to. But it wasn't to be. As he predicted, Ella stood on the other side, waiting for them to arrive. She jumped up from where she sat on the floor playing with her dolls.

"Papa!" she shouted, then ran toward them. He placed his wife carefully on the floor. Ella stared at her new mother, then looked her over, scanning every inch of her. "Is this my new Mama?" she asked, her voice almost hysterical, tears rolling down her cheeks.

Simon squatted down, then reached for his daughter and pulled her to him. "It is," he said with all the strength he could muster. He turned her to face his wife. "Ella, meet your Mama."

Lillian stared down at Ella and Simon, who were still squatting together on the floor. She had been determined this child would mean nothing to her and would not let Ella into her heart. Of course, she would look after her and do all the motherly things that were expected of her, but she would not let the little girl penetrate her heart.

At least that's what she decided at Hillier's Creek. It seemed a lifetime ago now. She'd lost far too many people she'd loved, and worried if this marriage didn't work out, how would she cope with losing the sweet girl standing in front of her?

When she glanced into Ella's face, her heart softened. A shudder went through her, and she knew her previous resolve had melted away. She was such a sweet little girl, and the look on her face – one of pure joy – at meeting her was more than she could endure. She squatted down to their level and opened her arms. Ella ran into them, almost knocking her over. But she didn't care. The child needed a mother more than anything in the world, and Lillian was determined to be that and more.

By now Ella was sobbing into her shoulder, and to her dismay, Lillian realized she, too, was sobbing. Tears flooded her face, and her heart was racing. It had to be the events of the past days causing it. There was no other valid reason. She had been through so much, and now to see such a sweet child so overwhelmed with joy, it had opened up the floodgates for her too.

She felt a gentle hand on her shoulder and glanced up. Simon stood above the pair, offering his handkerchief to her. She accepted it gratefully. Lillian slowly stood, bringing Ella up with her as she wiped her tears away. What a mess she must look. And on her wedding day too!

If her mother could see her now, she would say crying on your wedding day is a bad omen. But Lillian felt the contrary. Simon seemed genuinely concerned about her, and Ella… she needed a mother.

Truth be told, Lillian needed them both.

Martha had been ever so kind. She'd made up the spare bed for Lillian in case she decided to spend some time there. The two were complete strangers and the last thing on Lillian's mind was giving herself to a man she barely knew. She was uncertain of what she wanted at this point, and Simon wasn't pushing her either way, which she truly appreciated. Besides, she still hadn't told him her true identity.

Simon carried her luggage to the spare room and installed it in the small cupboard there. By doing so, he had made Lillian's decision for her. Did that mean he didn't want her in his bed? According to his letters, he wanted an heir. At least a handful of boys were on his agenda for their future, but she wasn't sure how that could be achieved if they slept in separate beds. Hopefully, it was a short-term situation, otherwise, she saw absolutely no point in her even coming here.

As she unpacked her few belongings, Lillian felt as though there were eyes on her, but when she turned around, she saw no one. She turned her back again, and the feeling returned. This time, she quickly spun around, and sneaking a peek at her around the door frame was young Ella. The child giggled at her trick, and Lillian couldn't help but join in. She opened her arms, and the little girl ran into them.

"Martha told me this your room now." She peeked inside Lillian's now empty case before glancing up at her new Mama.

What could she say to that? If she changed her mind, how did she explain it to a child of almost five years old? She wasn't certain she could. As she opened her mouth to speak, heavy footsteps came closer. Suddenly, the doorway was taken up by Simon as he watched them.

"Papa!" Ella squealed, then ran into his arms. Simon scooped her up and held the child closely. Lillian thought back to when she was in his arms not so very long ago. It had felt good, comforting, and she'd felt very safe and protected. So why on earth had she agreed to sleep in the spare room? Without so much as a word, she removed her meagre belongings from within the cupboard and placed them back in her near-threadbare bag.

His eyes followed her every move, but he said not a word. Not until she lifted the almost weightless bag and headed toward the doorway, where he stood. His head tilted to the side, his expression dark. "You're leaving? What about El…"

She reached up and put her fingers to his lips. His face had gone white, and he simply stared down at her.

"Where is *our* bedroom?" she asked, then watched a slow smile cross his face. Too late, she realized she spoke too soon. What if they consummated their marriage, and he annulled it when he found out who she really was? Or wasn't.

His daughter glanced from one to the other of them, not understanding what was happening. With one hand still around Ella, he reached down and took Lillian's hand in his. His fingers curled around hers, and her heart fluttered. She felt close to Simon already, and they'd been together for such a short period of time.

As she'd read his letters on the stagecoach, she could tell his heart was full of love and kindness, but she still didn't expect this. From the moment Joy had begged Lillian to take her place, she worried. She'd heard of mail order brides being abducted and worse on their way to their new homes. She'd read news articles about brides being killed or attacked by their new husbands, wife beaters, no less. All of that concerned her, but once she read the letters, her mind was put at ease.

His actions told her even more about this man who was now her husband than those letters ever would.

Lillian followed along as Simon pulled her toward the master bedroom. It wasn't far from the spare bedroom and also wasn't far away from Ella's room. There were several bedrooms, no doubt for all the heirs the Watson men expected to sire. Finally, he pulled her into the room, bouncing Ella onto the bed.

"Here we are," he said, a certain determination in his voice.

She didn't fail to see the sly smile that crossed his lips. He opened the wardrobe and revealed the half empty space. "I cleared this out for you yesterday," he said, not looking at her while he spoke. "Martha has promised to stay on for a week or two while you learn the run of things."

She swallowed down her nerves, knowing she would be totally alone the moment Martha walked out that door, especially this close to Christmas. "What about the workers? Am I charged with feeding them?" She was sure she already knew the answer before asking the question. Growing up on a ranch herself, she knew the decent employers supplied their men with good food. *Look after your workers, they look after you.*

And from all accounts, Simon seemed like a good and reasonable man.

He glanced down at her before scooping Ella up again. "That would be a yes," he said, then headed out of the bedroom before she had a chance to respond. At least she had a bit of a reprieve before Martha left her alone forever.

She stared out of the bedroom window and across the vast expanse of land owned by her handsome husband, then glanced at her marital bed. She sat on the side of the bed and prayed that her husband was gentle with her tonight. She also prayed they had a long and happy marriage, but knew for that to happen, she had to tell him who she really was.

It was a conversation she dreaded. *Would he send her back and have their marriage annulled?* Only time would tell.

Lillian stared as the cowboys all strolled into the kitchen one-by-one. They cleaned up on the porch, then headed inside to eat. All five of them.

Still, she should be grateful. There were far more workers on the ranch where her father had worked. They employed one cook and one dishwasher there, and nothing more. Of course, each family did their own cooking, but the single men were fed by old Clint, who owned the property. Lillian had a lot of time for the old man. He was a family man himself and had been cut up about the untimely death of his workers. He'd given their wives a month to find somewhere else to live before he inserted another family in each of the cottages. He'd even paid their husband's wages until they left.

She'd kept in contact with Clint until his death a few months ago – he had been kind to her family, and Lillian felt she owed it to him to keep in touch. His sons had taken over the ranch some years back. They had virtually grown up together, and she had a soft spot for the whole family as a result.

Martha dished out the soup and placed a bowl in front of each man, while Lillian placed two loaves of freshly baked bread in the center of the table. She glanced around at these strangers and wondered if she could live up to Martha's reputation. Sure, she could cook, but could she cook as well as Martha obviously could?

"That's my ride home," Martha said, as a buggy pulled up outside. "Enjoy your meal everyone." She reached for her thick shawl and wrapped it around her shoulders. The night air was crisp, and the last thing Lillian needed was for Martha to catch a chill and leave her alone to work it all out for herself.

Calls of goodnight rang around the table, and then Martha was gone.

Simon reached for her hand, and they bowed their heads in prayer.

"Lord," Simon said quietly but clearly. "Thank you, for this bountiful food set out before us. Also Lord, today we are joined by my wife Joy, but of course you know that. I pray she feels safe here, and settles in well. I pray also, she is a good mother to little Ella. Amen."

Lillian's heart thudded in her chest as Simon mentioned her cousin's name. What must the Lord be thinking about her now, pretending to be someone she wasn't? If it was the last thing she did, Lillian would tell her husband the truth. He needed to know exactly who he had married, and he needed to know before they consummated their marriage tonight.

He squeezed her hand, then let it go to eat his meal. He turned to face Lillian. "Let me introduce you to everyone. You already met Tucker – he's our foreman. And this is Hank, Joel, Bart, and Earl." He indicated each man as he spoke. "Fellas, this is my wife, Joy."

Lillian wanted to sink down from her chair and onto the floor. Not only did she have to tell her husband the truth, but these men as well. Not to mention Martha. Truth be told, they might not even be legally married. Her parents thought it was amusing to call her Lillian Joy, when her slightly older cousin was Joy Lillian. So she might get away with it. At least legally, but what would Simon think? Particularly if their marriage wasn't legal? Had she turned him into a criminal without his knowledge?

She groaned inwardly, then brought her spoon up to her mouth. She didn't enjoy the food because of the unpleasant taste in her mouth. It was of her own doing. She should have told Simon the moment they met. She'd intended to, but then thought he might send her back home, and that was the last thing she needed. Horace would be waiting on the side-lines for her; she knew he would. The vile man would like nothing better than to have her so vulnerable she would have no choice but to marry him.

She shuddered at the mere thought of it.

"It's very tasty," Lillian managed, knowing it was yet another a lie to pass her lips. She was certain if she didn't feel so terrible right now, it would be delicious, as her husband had said. Lillian glanced around the table – the men certainly seemed to be enjoying Martha's creation. They had almost finished, and she'd barely begun.

Simon glanced down at her bowl. He leaned in close. "Are you all right?" he whispered, and she nodded. It wasn't exactly the truth; she was feeling guilty about what she'd done, and nothing more. The sooner the truth came out, the better. As she swallowed down the last mouthful, it felt like she was trying to swallow razor blades. She reached for some water and gulped it down.

The meal seemed to go on forever. Martha had cooked a roast lamb in her honor and made apple pie for dessert. It had been dished out and was sitting on the counter for Lillian to distribute to everyone. Of course, there was coffee afterwards, and by the time they finished their meal, she was exhausted. She wanted nothing more but to crawl into bed and go to sleep. For the next one hundred years – that way she wouldn't have to face her husband and admit she was a bare-faced liar. It took all her effort not to blurt it out right now, but he deserved better. She had to wait until everyone was gone, and tell him in private.

By the time the last of the men left, Lillian was beyond exhausted. She felt like she was on death's door, but of course, that was not true. She'd spent days on the stagecoach and had not had a rest since she'd arrived at her new home. Everything was overwhelming and contributing to her exhaustion. The dishes hadn't been done yet, but she had no energy to wash them. Simon convinced her to leave them until morning. It went against everything she'd ever been taught, but what choice did she have? She was drained beyond anything she'd ever felt before, and had to get to sleep.

She could barely lift her feet, and felt herself being lifted into her husband's arms. She was asleep before they even left the kitchen.

Chapter Four

Lillian woke up in a daze. She glanced about but didn't recognize where she was. Until he spoke.

"Good morning." Simon's fingers grazed her arm as she tried to wake up properly. She glanced up to see him grinning at her. "You really were tired last night. I ended up carrying you to bed."

Bed! She was in his bed! Did that mean...

She surely would have remembered something like that, but she couldn't remember a moment beyond heading to bed after supper. "Did we…" She let the question hang, and he chuckled, his eyes full of mischief. It made her worry, since Lillian had wanted to tell him the truth.

"No, we didn't. You couldn't even stand up."

She felt enormous relief at his answer, since she wanted her husband to be fully aware of who she truly was before they consummated their marriage. She owed him that much, at least. After all, it wasn't Lillian he'd corresponded with – it was her cousin Joy. "There's something I need to tell you," she said, glancing up at him as he hovered above her in the bed. Even in bed, he seemed overly large, but he was only half sitting up, staring down at her.

"We could use the time more productively," he said, then sent her a cheeky grin. Suddenly, the door flew open, and a flash flew past Lillian and landed on the bed.

Simon sighed.

"Mama, Papa!" Ella shouted as she bounced on the bed.

And just like that, the moment was lost. *Would she never get to confess to her husband?* To declare the truth really was a confession. She knew it, and he would too once he heard her story. "We need to talk," she almost spat out, her plea sounding desperate now.

Holding his daughter against his chest, Simon stared at her and frowned. Surely he could sense the importance of her plea. The circumstances were becoming dire, at least to Lillian. Once they… well, she didn't want to leave it that long. Just the thought of their coming together sent heat into her cheeks.

As if he could read her thoughts, he grinned. Did he know what she was thinking? That surely wasn't possible. He leaned in and kissed her cheek, lingering a little too long. He had a hand to his daughter's back, holding her in place as though he were professing his love for them both. But, of course, Simon had no such feelings for her. Perhaps one day he might think that way, but today it was impossible. It was less than twenty-four hours since she'd arrived in Samson's Creek and it was not only highly unlikely for him to have feelings for her this quickly; it was impossible.

The man didn't even know who she really was, for goodness' sakes!

Lillian pulled herself to the edge of the bed, but before she could stand, felt tiny arms snake around her neck. *What if Simon rejected her once he knew the truth? Where would that leave little Ella? Would she be motherless again? The big question was, would he send her away, or banish her to the spare room?* The latter was the most likely scenario since he wouldn't want to let his daughter down, or upset her after finally securing a mother for her. Lillian's heart thudded in her chest. No matter what happened, it was a difficult situation for them all, but especially Ella.

She reached up and covered Ella's hands with her own. They were tiny compared to hers, and ever so soft. Before she knew what was happening, her step-daughter kissed her cheek. It was more than Lillian could take, and she felt unexpectedly overwhelmed, tears flooding her face. "Mama is crying," Ella shouted, suddenly distressed. "What's wrong Mama? Did I do something wrong?"

She shook her head, too overwhelmed to speak in that moment. Ella most definitely didn't do anything wrong. In fact, she'd done everything right, and it was just too much to take in. Finally, she managed to compose herself. "No, sweetheart. You didn't do anything wrong. On the contrary."

Simon pulled her against himself, bring Ella closer as well. "I think Mama is happy to be here," he said gently, staring into her face, his expression silently questioning her. Lillian didn't trust herself to get the words out without breaking into a sob, and simply nodded.

This man, this stranger, was comforting her. It was the last thing Lillian expected, but she rested her head against his chest regardless and listened to her husband's racing heart. What he must think, she couldn't fathom. She did, however, know it felt good to be in his arms, even if he only did it to comfort her in front of his child.

Ella suddenly jumped up. "Martha is here!" she shouted, and then she was gone, leaving the newlyweds alone.

"What's all this about?" he asked gently, his hand caressing her hair. "Not having second thoughts, I hope?"

She shook her head. "Nothing like that. I'm feeling more than a little overwhelmed, I guess. And... there's something I need to tell you."

"So you said." His words were curious now. They were also gentle. Any other man would probably be far less than patient with her.

"It's about the letters."

Ella was suddenly on top of the bed again. "Martha is bringing you a cup of tea," she whispered. "It's a surprise because you are crying."

Lillian was devastated. Ella told Martha, and now she would feel forever embarrassed in front of the housekeeper. Of course Ella wasn't even five yet, and it wouldn't occur to a child of that age that things like that were private.

Simon pulled her a little closer, hugging her tight. "Martha is a kind person. She wouldn't want you to be upset. And neither do I." He leaned in and kissed her forehead as the housekeeper entered the room with a cup of tea. She placed it on the side-table, and without so much as a word, left them alone.

"Drink your tea," Simon told her gently, passing it across to her. "I'll come and check on you a little later." He climbed out of bed, pulled on his trousers and shirt, then hurried out of the room.

Lillian suddenly felt hollow without him there with her. Her husband was a kind man, and someone she knew she could come to love, given time. She already had a soft spot for his daughter, and from what she'd seen of the ranch so far, she loved it here already. The last thing she wanted was to be sent away. She should resign herself to that happening, or at the very least, being banished to the spare room for the rest of her years. Of course, she would occasionally be allowed in the master bedroom – but only long enough for them to produce heirs to the Watson name.

She deserved nothing less. After all, Lillian was an impostor bride, and she knew it. Soon Simon would too.

It seemed like forever until Joy joined them in at the breakfast table, but Simon was willing to give her time. Everything was new to her, and she was obviously feeling overwhelmed. If he was in her shoes, a mail order bride who had traveled to a groom she had never met, wouldn't he feel the same? He knew he would.

The world was a scary place, and yes, they had corresponded with each other, but it wasn't the same as meeting in person. Joy didn't seem like the woman in her letters, but he hadn't known her long enough to get a true picture of what she was like. Besides, she was exhausted from her long days of travel.

One thing he knew for certain – Ella adored his wife. It appeared the feeling was mutual, as Joy seemed to love the child already. But what was there not to love? Ella was a sweet child, all credit to Martha, who had virtually brought her up. Martha and her husband were childless, which had been to his benefit, but he felt for them. He couldn't imagine his life without his daughter.

"Good morning." Joy's sweet voice rang out across the room, and every man turned his head to face her. He watched as each one broke into a smile. She seemed to light up the entire room, and he felt a ping of jealously. Simon shook the thought away – these men, his loyal workers, were not interested in his wife. They just enjoyed her company as he did.

Ella darted across the room, flinging herself at Joy, almost knocking her off her feet. "Mama!" she yelled as they connected. She hugged Joy's legs for the longest time, and Simon strode toward her, picking his daughter up.

"You almost knocked Mama over. Please be more careful."

His wife glanced up at him and her lips curled slightly. She seemed... he wasn't sure what, but something was bothering her, eating away at her, he was certain. Whatever it was she wanted to talk to him about was obviously upsetting his wife. He needed to make the time to sit down with her and sort it out. He would make time tonight after supper.

"Thanks for breakfast, Martha. Right boys, time for work."

Tucker stood, and the rest of the workers drank down the last of their coffee and pushed back their chairs, then strolled out the door.

"I should go too," he said, giving his daughter a hug. When he glanced up again, sadness was evident in his wife's eyes. Whatever was worrying her was deep-seated, and they needed to sort it out sooner rather than later. He put Ella to the floor, then stepped toward Joy, but she took two steps back. His heart thudded at the rejection. Instead of letting it anger or upset him, he opened his arms, and after hesitating momentarily, she stepped into them and rested her head against his chest, standing with her arms by her sides.

Finally, she relaxed against him and reached up, wrapping her arms around his body. Whatever was eating at her, he needed to vanquish it. Surely he could fix whatever ailed her? If his wife was unhappy, Simon was unhappy, and surely it would eventually rub off on Ella too? He pulled her a little closer, and she didn't resist.

His heart pounded as a number of scenarios flashed through his mind. Could she have already been married and didn't want to tell him? He could put up with a lot, but not that. Or maybe she carried another man's child? Simon immediately dismissed that thought – he'd seen the way she blushed when she stared at their marital bed. Whatever it was, he had to get to the bottom of it, and soon.

Without warning, she pushed away from him. "You have work to do. I won't keep you."

He stared down into her face. It was etched in pain. He didn't want to leave her like this; it was the last thing he wanted to do. "I can stay awhile." He pulled her toward himself again, but she resisted.

Her eyes filled with tears, and he watched as she fought them back. "No. I'll be fine. I won't be the wife that keeps you from your work." She pulled away again and hurried toward the front door and out of sight. *How was he expected to work with such a heavy mind?*

For a moment he was planted where he stood, then, finally coming to his senses, rushed after her, determined to get to the heart of the problem.

Simon stared momentarily as his wife sat on the edge of the porch, looking ahead, deep in thought. His heart broke realizing something was troubling her, but not knowing what it was. What could be so terrible that it almost brought her to tears? He approached, trying not to startle her, then sat down next to her. Joy's feet dangled in mid-air, and they swung as though it was the only thing keeping her sane. He reached out and wrapped his arm around her shoulders. "It's not that bad, is it?"

She lifted her head momentarily and glanced sideways at him. Her eyes were red and swollen, proving she was far more upset than he'd originally thought. "It's worse," she mumbled, turning her head away from him. He gently squeezed her shoulder, then pulled her a little closer.

"Joy," he said quietly, but she didn't respond. "Joy," he repeated, only a little louder this time.

She turned her head to the side and stared at him for only a moment then turned away again. She was blinking back tears, but despite all her efforts, failed. Tears ran down her cheeks and she brushed them away. He pulled a handkerchief from his pocket and held it out to her. Simon wasn't used to crying women and had no idea how to deal with the situation. He could ask Martha what to do, but knew he needed to deal with this himself – right now. Joy was, after all, his wife. His hand roamed over her back, trying to soothe her pain, whether that be physical or emotional. Either way, it was breaking his heart to see her like this. He worried it would become a daily occurrence if they didn't sort out the problem, and that was the last thing he wanted. For either of them.

Finally, in desperation, he raised his voice. "Joy, look at me!" Simon felt bad speaking in such a manner. He needed to get her attention.

No matter, it worked, and she sat straight and glanced his way. Tears continued to roll down her cheeks, and he was sorely tempted to pull her close and comfort his wife, but decided that wasn't what she needed right now. She needed a firm hand, and he must find out what it was that had caused so much distress.

Her eyes wide, she glared at him momentarily, then her face softened. "I'm not Joy," she said slightly above a whisper.

Now it was his turn to be astonished. *Not Joy?* Then who had he married if not Joy Hanover – the woman he'd been corresponding with for some time. "I don't understand," he finally answered, all the time watching her closely. His heart pounded in his head as well as his chest, and his head spun with the possibilities.

"Mama!" Ella came running out of the house toward them, Martha close on her heels. He watched as Joy, or whoever this woman was, turned her head away from his daughter. She swiped the tears from her face, then stood.

"I'm sorry," Martha said apologetically. "I tried to keep her inside."

He hugged the little girl, then carried her inside. "Stay here with Martha for a little bit," he told her. "While Mama and I talk."

"Can't I talk too?"

How did you explain to a child this young that some things needed to be kept between adults? "Maybe later," he said, glancing up at Martha. She nodded, and he knew his daughter would be contained in the house.

When he returned to where he'd sat with the woman he'd called Joy, she was gone. He glanced about and noticed her standing by the fence, hugging one of the oldest horses on the property. Bella had been his father's favorite. Though beyond doing anything meaningful, he didn't have the heart to part with her. She was happy enough, just too old to be put to work now.

He plodded toward the pair and put an arm around his wife's shoulder. It was then a thought struck him – if this wasn't Joy, were they legally married? "This is Bella," he said quietly, carefully avoiding the subject at hand. "She likes the occasional ride, if you ever feel inclined." Joy glanced across at him and nodded, then ran her hands up and down the horse's face, from her nose to her forehead.

"My name is Lillian," she breathed. "Joy is my cousin."

He stood gaping at the woman he had believed to be his wife. "So we're not really married?" He didn't know what to think, except it was probably serendipity that kept them from consummating their marriage the previous night. "And Joy? Why didn't she come as planned?" His head was pounding now, and he guessed the reason didn't matter so much as what they did next.

She took a deep breath, then let it out slowly. "I'm Lillian Joy Hanover, she is Joy Lillian Hanover. I have no idea if that makes a difference to the legalities of our marriage." She hugged Bella again. It seemed the presence of the horse calmed her. "She decided at the last minute not to come, said she fell in love with someone after she'd accepted your proposal. I needed to leave in a hurry as my vile boss was *harassing* me."

He stared at her. *Did she mean what he thought she meant?* Men who behaved that way should be flogged. Simon felt the anger building up inside him. As though she sensed his anger, she lifted a hand and ran it down his jaw.

"He didn't do anything," she hissed. "I was able to keep him at arm's length. But I don't know how much longer I could have done that. I had to leave quickly. The plan was to tell you the moment I stepped off the stagecoach. I didn't intend on being as exhausted as I was. I couldn't think straight."

It explained a lot and was likely the reason she didn't answer when he called her name. Or should he say Joy's name? He wasn't sure what to say, so nodded his acknowledgement of her words.

"I'm sorry, I really am," she murmured, and looked as though she would burst into tears again. Simon pulled her close against him, his arms wrapped tightly around her. He didn't want to lose her – in the short time they'd been together, he already had feelings for her. What they did to fix the problem was the question, and she was surely wondering, too.

"We'll sort it out. I don't know how, but we'll find a way to fix it." His grip on her tightened even more. "That is, if you want to stay married to me."

She glanced up and gazed into his eyes. "I do, but after my appalling deception, is that what you want?"

He studied her face for what seemed forever and fought back the emotion that threatened to surface. *Was that what he wanted?* Without hesitation, Simon knew the answer.

Chapter Five

Ella sat between them as they made their way into town. This time Lillian took in the scenery and drank it in. She was beyond exhausted when she'd originally arrived. It was the reason she hadn't told Simon who she really was. The little girl held Lillian's hand tightly, and she had a big grin on her face.

"She doesn't get to town very often," Simon said. "I didn't have the heart to leave her home today."

"You must be excited," Lillian told her step-daughter, forcing a smile onto her face. *Could they fix this, or would they have to marry again? Was that even possible since they'd married already, but with Lillian using her cousin's name?* She wondered if Simon really did want to marry her, or if he felt obligated. She reached across and placed her hand over his. "You don't have to do this, you know." She studied him and his smile turned into a tight line.

He glanced at her momentarily. "I want to do it. I know we haven't been together long, but I already have feelings for you."

She felt the same about Simon, but also worried about Ella if she left. *How would the little girl cope with losing her new Mama so soon?*

"We're almost there," he said, pointing toward the church steeple that was just coming into sight. "This is totally your decision. If you've changed your mind, tell me now. Otherwise it will be too late."

"I want to be married to you," she breathed, and her heart fluttered at the thought.

They pulled up outside the church, and Simon climbed off the wagon and helped her down. Then Ella jumped into his arms. "Remember what I said? You need to sit quietly in church while we talk to Preacher Joe."

"I remember, Papa." She skipped ahead and waited at the heavy door to enter. Lillian's heart quivered as they stepped inside, wondering what the outcome would be. *Would the preacher say they couldn't marry, or would he void their original marriage on the spot?* As she made her way down the aisle of the church, Lillian felt as though she was walking toward doom.

"Good morning! How is married life treating you both?" The preacher's voice boomed down the building. He was obviously delighted to see them, but what would he think when he found out the reason for this visit. "Miss Ella. I am delighted to see you. You've grown so much." He grinned at the child, and she beamed at his words.

"I growed very big," she said, fully animated now.

"What can I do for you today?" the preacher asked. Curiosity crossed his face now. "I hope everything is all right?"

Simon picked Ella up and placed her on the front pew, reminding her of her promise to sit quietly. "Is there somewhere we can talk?"

Preacher Joe glanced from Simon to Lillian, and unease seemed to cross his face. "Of course. Follow me." He led them to a small room at the side of the church, where he counseled his parishioners. "I'll leave the door ajar so we can hear that Ella is all right. Sit yourselves down." He indicated the two chairs opposite a lone chair, which was obviously meant for the preacher.

Lillian was apprehensive about the entire situation. *What if they were deemed to be unmarried with no way of fixing the problem, and she had to return home?* Her back stiffened, knowing she could never return to Boise. Not while Horace Periwinkle was there. The man had all but seduced her in the storeroom that last day. She couldn't risk that happening again. If things were that dire, she would have to rethink her situation.

She was suddenly aware of Simon explaining the predicament they found themselves in, his voice low so Ella couldn't hear. Preacher Joe glanced across at Lillian, his expression solemn. "I'm sure you didn't mean to deceive either Simon or the church," he said with a slight edge to his voice.

Lillian couldn't bear to look at him, and glanced down into her lap instead. "No, Sir, I did not. Everything happened so quickly, and I…" She lifted her head to look at him. "To be brutally honest, I was exhausted and couldn't even think straight."

Preacher Joe reached out and patted her hand. "I'm sure there's a way to fix this prickly problem." He put a hand to his chin and tapped it. Then he squeezed his eyes tightly closed. "Wait here," he said. "I won't be but a moment." He left them alone, but soon returned. He was only gone long enough for Simon to cover Lillian's hand with his own.

"This," the preacher said, holding a large book, "is the marriage registry. Oh look," he said, mock surprise in his voice. "I must have written your name incorrectly, Mrs. Watson." When she glanced at him over the use of her married name, Lillian noticed the elderly preacher winking. "I'll have to issue a new marriage certificate, though. When you return home, you must destroy the incorrect one."

He scribbled something on the registry, which Lillian assumed was him making corrections to her name, and then he stood. "What a wonderful day it is," he said cheerfully as he stood. "The sun is shining, and I have a wonderful family visiting me. Do you have plans for the day?"

Simon stood and shook the preacher's hand. "Thank you, Preacher. You have allayed my greatest fear – that I would lose my precious wife."

Lillian was surprised at the emotion she heard in his voice.

"Have no fear, my son. All is well with the world." He clapped Simon on the back, then walked over to little Ella. "You have been such a good girl." He reached into his pocket and pulled out a small paper bag. "I keep these bags of sweets for well behaved children such as yourself."

She glanced up at Simon, who nodded his approval, then Ella reached out and took the offered treat. "Thank you Preacher Joe," she whispered, a grin on her face.

"Thank you for everything," Simon echoed. "We both appreciate everything you've done for us."

As they walked back down the aisle toward the entrance to the church, Lillian's heart felt a little lighter.

Ella pushed the food around her plate without eating so much as a mouthful. She pouted as she stared at her father. "I don't want this," she growled. "I want cake." Her little eyes opened wide in astonishment as her father scowled at her, but to Lillian's amazement, he didn't scold the little girl.

"Eat your fish, and I'll think about it." He spoke quietly, then turned to his wife and winked. This meal was meant to be their wedding celebration. A little late since the original wedding day had passed, but knowing they were still legally married was definitely a reason to celebrate.

Lillian picked up her mug of coffee and sipped it, trying to hide her smile. The last thing she wanted to do was undermine Simon's authority over the child. But from what he'd told her, he'd had little contact with Ella except for late evenings once Martha left to go home. By that point, she was fed, bathed, and in her nightgown, ready for sleep. All he had to do was read her a bedtime story and settle her down to sleep. If he arrived home late, she was often already asleep, and he didn't get to see her that day at all.

That was no way for Simon to have a meaningful relationship with his daughter, and she hoped to change that.

Ella scowled back at her papa, then grinned and filled her mouth with fish. This would be the first time Lillian had seen any sort of rebellion from the little girl, and it made her wonder. *Did Ella understand what it meant that she and Simon had married? Was this a protest of sorts?* Lillian felt it was, but had no idea how to deal with it. For now, she would leave it to Simon to sort out. After all, she didn't want to overstep her place in the household. This was all so new to her, and to be honest, she wasn't certain what was expected of her.

Did her husband want or even expect her to discipline Ella? Would it even be needed? She had no answers to any of these questions and needed to discuss it with Simon. They'd begun on very shaky ground, so she wasn't convinced he would be happy for her to even spend time alone with Ella, let alone want her to discipline the girl. She had no experience with children, so how could he even trust she could look after his daughter appropriately? The bottom line was that he couldn't. Lillian wasn't convinced herself that she could. The only way toward a solution was to talk to Martha, and hopefully the housekeeper would have some advice to provide.

"I finished all my fish," Ella proudly announced, her eyes wide in expectation. "Can I have cake now?"

She was such a sweet little girl, and Lillian could feel her excitement. She knew Simon had other things planned for their day in town, and hoped Ella would last the distance. She was, after all, four going on five.

Simon beckoned for the waitress and ordered three slices of cake.

"You're spoiling us," she said, meaning every word. Lillian couldn't even remember how long it had been since she'd eaten out, let alone had cake.

His hand snaked across the table and squeezed hers. "Both my girls are worth it." His words rang through her mind. He'd included her as part of his family, and that, more than anything else, had made her feel as though she belonged. She swallowed back the emotion that was making its way through her.

It had been a very long time since Lillian felt she'd fitted in. Even with her cousin Joy – they'd once been very close but had drifted apart with time. That had been proven with the way Joy had deceived her, to convince Lillian to take her place. As far as she was aware, there was no boyfriend, no Timothy Chambers. Boise was a small town, and if there'd been such a person, she would surely have known of his existence.

The truth of the matter was, Joy had tricked her into taking her place once she found out she would have to mother someone else's child. It was a despicable thing to do, but even more despicable knowing she'd already accepted Simon's marriage proposal. Worse still was the fact she had agreed to this appalling plan. The guilt she'd felt was overwhelming, and she knew it wouldn't be relieved until she'd told Simon the truth. She was more than a little grateful that he was an understanding and patient man.

"Yummy!"

She'd been so tied up in her own thoughts, Lillian hadn't heard the waitress return. Ella's excitement at seeing the cake brought her back to the present.

"It does look delicious," Simon told them both after he'd thanked the waitress. Carrot cake had always been a favorite of hers, and it looked like her new family liked it too. Perhaps she could make a cake in the coming days?

Simon seemed like a man who loved his food, and what she'd seen so far had proven that. She would ensure baking became a regular part of her week. Ella would probably enjoy helping with the baking, too. She had no idea if Martha ever let the girl help with the baking, and it got her to wondering what Ella did with her day. Lillian had no idea if she even had many toys. She would buy all the toys in the world if it made Ella happy, but then she remembered she had little money. Only the few coins left over from the expenses Simon had provided. If she was being honest, she should hand that money over to him, even if it wasn't much. With that thought in her mind, she opened her reticule, and handed over the loose coins she found there.

He stared into her hand. "What is this?"

"The left-over money from the expenses." She squinted at him as though daring him to refuse.

That's exactly what he did. "Keep it, I don't need it."

"Neither do I. At least I don't think I do." Now she was confused. It was all the money she had in the entire world. Should she even be offering back to Simon? "Or do I?"

"You don't. Anything you need can go on my account at any of the stores in town. But if it makes you feel better, keep those coins, and I'll give you more to go with them."

Was he mocking her now? Lillian was confused. She couldn't tell if he was joking or was being serious. Apart from customers in Horace's store, she'd had little exposure to men, and had no idea how to read them.

She stared down into her hand and the coins, then tucked them back into her well-worn reticule. It wasn't long before they finished the cake and headed outside. Simon took them to the mercantile and bought a new dress for a very excited Ella. He also let her pick out a new toy, which turned out to be a rag doll, then told Lillian to choose something for herself.

She was reluctant at first, but he insisted and told her he'd be insulted if she didn't. Lillian wasn't convinced, but chose something anyway. She held a cotton nightgown away from herself and studied it. It was soft pink, with tiny bows down the front, complimented by small ribbon flowers.

"It will look real pretty on you," he whispered in her ear. "Not that you'll get to wear it for long."

Lillian felt heat rise in her cheeks and turned to stare at him, a scowl on her face. He towered over her and laughed.

"It's true," he said, then kissed her cheek before putting an arm around her and pulling her against him.

She rested her head against his chest and listened to his strong and steady heartbeat. Simon's arms came up around her, his strength seeping into her, and Lillian relaxed against him. The world around them disappeared, and it was as though only the two of them existed. Lillian knew she shouldn't be doing this, especially in the middle of the mercantile. People were likely staring at them, but right now, at this moment in time, she didn't care. After everything she'd endured over the past days, she simply wanted to be here in her husband's arms, feeling wanted and loved.

Was this what life with Simon would be like? She hoped so, because she was beginning to enjoy being his wife.

The trip home was far easier than the one into town. Simon's heart felt much lighter, and for a minute there, he thought he would lose Lillian and Ella would lose her mother. The two had already hit it off, and he knew he'd made the right choice for his wife.

That thought made him pause, because Lillian wasn't the wife he chose, although she did seem to be the wife he needed. He knew he should be fuming at the switch the two women had made, but right now, he was thankful his marriage to Lillian was legal. He couldn't think of anything worse than believing they were married, only to find out they weren't. It sounded strange to him, but Simon was grateful they hadn't consummated their marriage before today. Otherwise he might have been frantic, thinking he'd broken one of the commandments, even if he wasn't aware of the deception.

He'd been brought up to be a good Christian, and he would have been heartbroken if he'd inadvertently done the wrong thing. He glanced across at his wife. Ella had finally stopped fighting sleep, and her head lay across her mother's lap. She looked so peaceful laying there with not a care in the world. Which was exactly how a child should be. Children should never been burdened with adult problems. Not ever.

"It's so peaceful here." Lillian's sweet voice brought him back to the present, and he smiled at the sound of her voice. His hand slid across and covered hers, and a shiver ran through him.

"It is. I love the tranquility of this area. As much as I don't like the travel, the serenity always gives me time to think." And it did. His thoughts were unclouded out here, and his troubles seemed to drop away. "I have time to contemplate what were previously insurmountable problems."

"And now?"

He turned to her and smiled. "And now they are no longer problems. Everything has fallen into place." All he needed now was for the two of them to learn to be friends, and then perhaps…

"I'm glad." Her words interrupted his thoughts again, and his heart thudded. Simon knew where his thoughts were heading. That perhaps one day they might fall in love. But he knew the reality was far from that. They would tolerate each other for their separate needs; for Lillian, it would be the safety of a husband and home. For Simon, it was for his wife to bear his heirs. Provided he understood that and kept it at the front of his mind, they could lead happy enough lives.

The most important thing was for little Ella to have a mother she could love and depend on.

Her hand landed gently on his arm, and Simon felt warmth fill him. Their short time together had already changed his life. Changed Ella's life. Lillian might have deceived him, but the fact she insisted on telling him the truth told Simon she was a good and honorable person. She was keen to talk to the preacher, which told him she was also a good Christian woman. That she'd lied to him to begin with still bothered him, but they would work through the challenges. He was sure they would.

He suddenly pulled the wagon to a stop, disturbing his daughter's sleep. Lillian squealed in fright, and Ella jumped up from her deep slumber. "Sorry," he said apologetically, although he had no control over what had occurred. "A deer ran out in front of us." He pulled on the brake, then jumped down from the buggy to assess if there was any damage. He had thankfully missed the animal.

He walked all around the buggy as the deer ran into the bushes. From his side vision, he watched as Lillian comforted his daughter. She now had the one thing his daughter had always craved but never had – the love of a mother. If nothing else ever came of this union, at least he knew his daughter would get all the love a child needed.

Martha had done the best she could, but she wasn't Ella's mother. Did he dare to think some of Lillian's love might ever come his way? He shook the thought away as he finished checking the buggy. As he'd hoped, there was no damage, and they could continue their trip home. Hopefully, with no further interruptions.

As always, supper was a community affair, with all the workers joining them for a beef stew Martha had made while they were out. The moment Lillian stepped inside the ranch house, she felt as though she'd come home. Not that it had been her home for long, but the aroma of food cooking seemed to be a beacon for her. It made her feel comforted, and she had no explanation for that. Although, as she thought back to her childhood, her mother always had something on the stove or in the oven. It might be a stew, or a roast, or even vegetable soup. The aroma of food cooking represented home to her. Lillian now realized it was the reason hadn't felt at home in her little rented room in Boise. She was barely home long enough to do much in the way of cooking, and what she did make was very basic.

"That was delicious, Martha." Tucker sang his praises as he always did at mealtimes, and Lillian wondered if he would do the same for her when she took over. She was nervous for the day when Martha left her alone, and not in a good way. The older woman promised to teach her what needed to be done, and Lillian had no doubt she would. She just wasn't convinced she would manage on her own.

"There's rhubarb and apple pie in the oven," she said, directing her words at Lillian. "The clotted cream is over here on the countertop."

Lillian nodded and watched as Martha removed her once pristine apron.

"How will I ever cope without you?" She was genuinely worried about when the housekeeper would leave her alone to do everything Martha had been doing for years.

"You'll manage, I know you will." She placed a firm hand on the younger woman's shoulder, exuding so much confidence, it almost rubbed off on Lillian. "Besides, I'll be here for a little longer."

Simon covered her hand with his own. "It will all work out, I'm certain. Martha won't leave us until you feel confident." He glanced up at Martha, who looked far from happy.

She'd promised two weeks at most, and Lillian had to honor that timeframe. Otherwise, it wouldn't be fair to the housekeeper, who had been more than generous already.

"I'm sure I'll be fine," she said, now studying the older woman. "Martha is a good teacher, and I'm a quick learner."

Martha's face relaxed a little, and she was soon on her way. The moment the men finished eating, Lillian collected all the soiled dishes, then handed out the pie, which Martha had already served into bowls. When she sat down again, her eyes swept over the men seated at the table, and she knew this was her life for the rest of her days. Feeding men she barely knew, but would one day know better than she knew herself.

They were all good men, and despite not knowing him well, was certain her husband would not employ anyone who was not a decent person, or a Christian. She should feel privileged to sit amongst them. Right now, Lillian wasn't sure what she felt.

Chapter Six

"Mama, Papa!" The little voice woke Lillian out of a deep sleep, the best she'd had for as long as she could remember.

Last night, she had become Mrs. Simon Watson in every way. More than anything, she was pleased they had waited until their marriage issues were sorted out, otherwise she knew she would feel incredibly guilty. Not to mention what it would have done to Simon. Yes, she definitely did the right thing.

As she glanced out the window, Lillian noticed the sun was just peeking above the horizon. Ella could be an early riser when she wanted to be. *Was it any wonder she napped in the middle of the day?* Not that she could complain – she would have been up shortly anyway, to get her husband's breakfast.

Well, get everyone's breakfast. Martha would arrive any moment, but Lillian thought it was probably time she pulled her weight and do the work she was brought here to do.

She gave Ella a quick hug, snatched up her clothes, then headed to the bathroom and a little more privacy. Glancing at herself in the small mirror, she groaned. Her hair was far more disheveled than normal, no doubt due to the antics of last night. Heat filled her cheeks just thinking about it.

The moment the thought entered her head, she admonished herself. It was, after all, the natural behavior of newlyweds. Now her cheeks were burning. Lillian splashed cold water on her face and quickly dressed, then fashioned her unruly hair into a temporary bun so she could get out into the kitchen. She wanted to beat Martha there, and prove she had it in her to feed the household.

She pulled two frying pans from the cupboard and placed them on the stove. There weren't enough eggs to cover this morning's meal, and she called her daughter. "Ella! Want to come with me to collect the eggs?"

She heard a squeal from the other room, then her new little daughter ran into the kitchen carrying her shoes. Once Lillian had helped her put on the shoes, they hurried out to the henhouse. "Have you collected eggs before?" she asked the child, as she carried a large bowl to place them in.

"I've helped Martha sometimes," she said carefully as she squeezed her eyes closed in thought. It made Lillian wonder how many times it had occurred.

"First, we open the door to let the hens out." She opened the door as she said the words. "Now stand back and let them get out."

Ella stood there with her eyes wide open in excitement, which made Lillian even more convinced she'd never collected the eggs before. Or at the very least, rarely collected them.

Suddenly, Ella rushed inside. Lillian grabbed the back of her dress, which she now noticed was inside out. Evidently, Ella hadn't dressed herself before. "Slowly and quietly, Ella. You don't want to frighten any hens that might still be inside." Ella nodded. "Now we need to find their nests and collect the eggs." She carefully reached into the high up nests and pulled out several eggs.

She held out the bowl for Ella to see. "If you promise to be careful, you can collect some, too. Be very gentle, otherwise they might break." She showed a nest where the child could easily reach. In her enthusiasm, she grabbed at the egg, moving it toward the bowl.

"Look!" she told Lillian excitedly, but held it too tight and it smashed in her hand. Her eyes opened in surprise, then she burst into tears.

Lillian squatted down to Ella's level and hugged her. "It's all right," she said. "It was an accident. Next time hold it gently." She wiped her tears away and indicated for her to take another egg from the nest. She carefully transported it to the bowl without incident. By the time they'd finished, there were more than a dozen eggs in the bowl. Plenty for breakfast, and enough left over for some baking.

Ella skipped ahead, then ran inside. She could hear the child's excited voice telling her father about her escapade in the chicken coup. It warmed Lillian's heart to know she'd made this little girl so happy, and to have filled a void in her short life.

If only she could do the same for her husband.

Simon turned as Lillian entered the house, his eyes scanning her from head to toe. Heat rose into her cheeks, and she turned away. Her husband strode toward her and enveloped Lillian in his arms. She leaned her head against his chest, listening to the strong and steady beat of his heart. She'd done that last night too, and it had felt comforting, much like it was doing right now.

Lillian tipped her head back and stared at his unshaven face. His eyes seemed to twinkle, and he winked at her. "I've been hearing all about your adventure with the chickens," he said, pulling her closer still.

"It was fun!" Ella sounded far more excited than Lillian had ever seen her, and it warmed her to think she was responsible for the little girl's joy. "Can we do it again?" She studied her Mama from the breakfast table as she waited for an answer.

"Not today, sweetheart," Lillian told the disappointed child. "There are no eggs left. But we can collect them again tomorrow."

"Yippee!"

"Now finish up your breakfast like a good girl."

Simon pulled her a little closer, then leaned in and kissed her gently on the lips. Lillian could get used to it, but knew it meant nothing to her husband, just like last night meant little to him. But for her, it was a totally different story. Lillian pretended Simon had feelings for her, that she was important to him. But deep in her heart, she knew it wasn't true. Men had cravings, and she was just a receptacle for those cravings. It wasn't as though he loved her. *How could he, after such a short time?* They were strangers and would remain that way for many months to come. The sooner she resigned herself to that fact, the better.

"Thank you," he whispered as he held her tight.

She glanced up into his face again. "For what?" What could she possibly have done to deserve his thanks?

"You've made our daughter happy. Ella hasn't been this happy for a very long time."

Not *my* daughter, but *our* daughter. She was still getting used to being a mother, and his words warmed her. If she let her guard down, Lillian knew the tears would flow, but she had no intention of becoming a blubbering mess in front of her husband. "All I did was take her to the henhouse. I felt sure she would have done it before." She glanced up questioningly at him, and Simon stared into her eyes. He moved his head slowly toward her, as though he was going to kiss her again, and time seemed to stand still.

"Martha!" Ella's high pitched squeal had Simon jumping back, his arms dropping from around her. The annoyance on his face matched the way she also felt.

"Good morning, Martha," Simon said, his voice flat.

When Lillian glanced across, Martha had a huge grin on her face. Did she think something had been going on between them? If so, then she'd be wrong. It didn't take long before Lillian realized *she* was wrong, not Martha. Simon had been holding her close and about to kiss her – again. He might not have any real feelings for her, but he seemed to enjoy holding and kissing her. She guessed any man would. Simply because she was female.

"We must plan our Christmas baking," Martha said as Lillian took her place in the kitchen. She placed the bowl of eggs on the countertop, then stared at the older woman. She hadn't given it a thought, not even once.

"What did you have in mind?" She'd done a lot of baking in her life, but never for such a large number of people.

"We definitely need a Christmas cake and a Christmas pudding, and I usually make mince pies as well. Which reminds me – I need to write up a list for the mercantile. They need plenty of time to get in all the supplies we'll need."

Lillian swallowed down her reservations over this entire situation. This year she would have help from Martha, but what about next Christmas? She would be completely alone. It would be a struggle with no one else to help. She helped Ella down from the table when she finished eating and cleaned the little girl up. Almost on cue, the workmen strolled into the house, ready for their morning meal.

Her attention now focused on the workers, Lillian set the table, ready for them to eat. Tucker grabbed up the mugs and poured the coffee for everyone, which was a tremendous help, while Martha finished cooking bacon and eggs. How she would manage all this on her own, Lillian had no idea. Never in her life had she needed to cater to so many people at once. She was merely a store assistant back home, and didn't do anything like this. Stacking shelves was the biggest part of her job, and she spent more time in the storeroom than out – much to Horace's delight.

The thought of that horrible man sent shivers down her spine. As though he sensed her dread, Simon put his arm across her shoulder. "Everything all right?"

The last thing she wanted to do was to talk about her former employer, particularly with everyone close at hand. Instead, she nodded. "I'm fine. But thank you for checking." As though she'd made his entire day, Simon's smile lit up his face, sending tentacles of delight running down her spine.

He leaned in and kissed her forehead, and warmth spread through her. Despite the fact there was no love between them, just being near Simon made her feel happy. Things could only get better. *Couldn't they?*

The meal over with, Lillian collected up the soiled dishes.

"Delicious meal," Tucker said as he headed for the front door. As they left one by one, each man thanked Martha for the meal. It was something she had to look forward to.

The moment they were gone, Simon pulled her close and kissed her on the cheek. "I have to go," he said, and there was a touch of sadness to his words. *Was he sad because he had to leave her, or before he would miss his daughter?*

Ella ran over and slammed into them. "Please don't go Papa!"

He leaned down and ruffled his daughter's hair. "I have to go to work. You know that." He glanced down at her, and Ella pouted.

"Please, Papa?"

Even her sad little eyes couldn't persuade him. "You know I can't." He reached down and picked her up. "I'll be back later – you know that. Now be a good little girl for Mama and Martha."

Still pouting, she nodded her head and wrapped her arms around his neck. As he was about to put her back to the floor, Ella gave him a big sloppy kiss, then suddenly pulled out of his grip and slid to the floor. "Goodbye, Papa," she said as she began to play with her dolls.

Simon chuckled. Ella was easily distracted, but in this instance, it worked to their advantage. He gave Lillian one last hug, then pulled out of her arms, seeming equally upset about leaving her. She would never know if his distress was genuine or whether he was putting on a show for his new wife.

Without another word, he was gone.

Lillian helped Martha bake bread, then they moved onto the laundry. It was a big job, since she was not only washing for her own family, but for all the workers as well. It was an arduous task, but one that had to be done. The sun was shining, but there was a certain chill in the air, and she wasn't sure the washing would even dry today. By mid afternoon it had come over so cold, they'd moved the washing to the ropes on the porch. There they would get the wind but were protected from the ice-chill of the elements. It was only mere weeks until Christmas, and dread had filled her. There had been no discussion of plans for Christmas, and Lillian worried there would be even more people to feed than usual. Martha rarely spoke unless she was spoken to, preferring to simply go about business. The biggest concern was the question that had been on Lillian's lips from the start – would she be able to take over this household and run it successfully.

After all, the success of the entire ranch depended on whether or not she could feed and take care of all the people living on this ranch, family or not.

As she made the beds, she thought about how she could move forward. Simon was such a kind man, but that wasn't enough for her. Lillian wanted more than kindness. She wanted him to feel something for her, like she felt for him.

The trouble was, they hadn't spent enough time together. They'd married then he'd gone back to work immediately. That same day, in fact. At least the first time they'd married. The second time, when they were genuinely married, they'd spent a few hours together, but it still wasn't enough. What she needed was days, not hours, but Lillian knew that wasn't about to happen. Simon had work to do, and orders to fulfil. The butcher had placed his order for Christmas, and Simon had to ensure the beef cattle would be ready on time. This was his busiest time of the year, he'd told her.

It made her wish she'd arrived earlier, because perhaps then they would have had additional time to spend together. However, if the arrangement had been for earlier, would she even have come here? Her cousin Joy might have taken the trip herself earlier in the year. She wouldn't have met the mysterious Timothy Chambers by then. Unless, of course, he was a figment of her cousin's imagination.

What if Joy had decided not to marry Simon because she didn't like the thought of becoming a mother to someone else's child? As much as she loved Joy, she had always been somewhat selfish. She wouldn't think about Simon, or Ella, she would only think of herself. The thought made her blood boil. *How dare she refuse to marry Simon because of a little girl who had absolutely no choice in the matter!*

She finished making the bed, then picked up the toys in Ella's room, placing them in a wooden box in the corner. She straightened the clothes in the child's cupboard, and opened the curtains, letting the light in, just as Simon and Ella had brought light into her life.

Despite the circumstances, and the deception, Lillian was more than delighted that she'd taken her cousin's place as Simon's mail order bride.

Chapter Seven

It was hard to believe they'd now been married for several days. Their previous difficulties were now behind them and were all but forgotten. Every morning they went through the same ritual, with Ella begging him to stay home, and Simon holding Lillian close as though he didn't want to leave. Which he didn't.

It wouldn't have been as much as three hours later when Simon returned home. Lillian was in the kitchen preparing a stew for supper, and Martha was making pastry. He loved knowing he would come home to find his wife waiting there for him.

Oh, he knew it was an old fashioned thought, since many women worked at an outside position these days. He was grateful Lillian didn't need to do that. He had a thriving ranch that more than covered costs, and he had a nice little nest-egg sitting in the bank should they ever need it.

Ella sat on the floor to the side of the kitchen, playing with her dolls. She glanced up as he opened the door.

"Papa!" She jumped up and ran to him, her arms opened wide. It was such a simple thing, but it sent warmth soaring through him. He lifted his daughter up into his arms and hugged her.

Lillian spun around and studied him. "Is everything all right?"

Did she think he was injured?

"I am perfectly fine. Can't I come and visit my girls?"

She squinted at him and studied him further. "I thought this was your busiest time of the year."

That's exactly what he'd told Tucker when he'd insisted they could do without him. "Blame Tucker." He couldn't help but grin at the bold statement.

"Tucker?" She was clearly confused.

"My foreman believes we need to spend some time together, getting to know each other."

With that, Martha abandoned the pastry and left the room, taking Ella with her. She always was discreet, which suited Simon just fine.

"Oh." Lillian wiped her hands on her apron and stepped toward him. "I'm in the middle of making a stew for supper."

"I can see." He glanced down at her and wiped a wisp of flour from her cheek. The motion made him want to kiss her. The pull was just too great, and he leaned down and covered her lips with his own. When he lifted his head, her cheeks were tinged with pink. "Perhaps we can go for a picnic, just the three of us."

"As a family. I'd like that." Her eyes lit up, and warmth flooded him. When he'd sent away for a mail order bride, he had no idea he would fall in love. His only thought was for someone to take over from Martha and to provide him with heirs. What a fool he'd been to think he could marry someone and not have feelings for her. Lillian had affected him almost from the moment she'd arrived. Even if he did think she was her cousin, Joy.

Things had turned out far better than he'd expected, and his heart was now filled with happiness. He stood holding his wife, and his heart pounded. Her hand came up and touched his cheek, and his heart fluttered. He felt like a teenage boy with his first crush. But he was a grown man, and he had no right having these feelings for someone he barely knew.

It was also what Tucker had told him, and now he understood what his foreman had tried to tell him. In fact, he could now appreciate the words he'd said. He had more than enough workers to fulfil the order, Tucker said, so he needed to just enjoy the time he had with his family.

His family.

They were a family now. Tucker was right. It had been so long that it was only Ella and himself. He hadn't given it much thought. But now with Lillian…

Did she have such thoughts about him? Simon guessed he would never know, but he wanted to give this marriage a chance to become real.

"I have blueberry muffins in the oven, and there's bread freshly baked. It should be cool enough to cut by the time we need it."

"I thought we could take the buggy down near the stream and spread a blanket out there. It's been a very long time since Ella has been on a picnic." He suddenly realized she'd never been on a picnic with her father, except for church picnics for the entire congregation. Never just the two of them. What a sad state of affairs.

Lillian finished the stew and put it on to cook, then busied herself getting ready for their picnic. Simon was surprised by the sense of excitement he experienced.

Ella's excitement level was far greater than anything Simon had seen from her before. She pointed out everything to Lillian – trees, flowers, horses, cows, and even the sun. It was amusing, but at the same time, almost distressing. His daughter had been deprived of her childhood, and all because he'd been too selfish to make the time for her.

Martha had done a wonderful job of raising her. But bringing his daughter up was his responsibility. His wife had died, and he'd been in mourning, but that was no excuse for not making the time for Ella. He would see her for such a short time in the mornings, then she was asleep when he arrived home. He had to do better. *Perhaps that's what Tucker was trying to tell him? Now that he had a new wife, it was a perfect time to change his ways?*

He certainly didn't want to alienate Lillian the way he'd done with his daughter. He wanted, no needed, to get to know them both. He barely knew his daughter, and the tragedy of it all was that meant she barely knew him. Was that what he wanted? For Ella to grow up not knowing her father? The mere thought of it made his heart thud.

"What's that hill called, Papa?" Ella said, bringing him back to the present. He followed the direction she indicated and smiled.

"That's Samson's Mountain. Named after your grand-papa." He thought about all the time he'd spent on that mountain with his own father, hunting deer for food. Never for pleasure, as some men did, and only ever enough to keep them fed. Memories came flooding back, and all of them good. He'd had a great childhood with his parents, and father had always made the time for him no matter how busy he'd been. Guilt overwhelmed him at the thought of having excluded Ella from his life all these years. It wasn't his daughter's fault her mother had died. *Had he unwittingly blamed her?* He hoped not.

"There Papa, there!" she screeched.

They'd arrived at the stream, and Ella wasn't going to let him miss it. The area was just as he'd remembered, jotted with Ponderosa Pine and Rocky Mountain Juniper. There was originally little space to sit, but together with his father, they'd cleared the area many years ago. It was a good fishing spot, and they'd used it often. This area was part of his land, but it was far too dense with trees to make it worthwhile for the cattle. Instead, he would come out here now and again with some of his men and collect firewood from fallen branches.

Ella squealed as she jumped down from the buggy, and it made him smile. "Stay close, and don't go near the water," he instructed, and Ella pouted.

He helped Lillian down, then laid the picnic blanket on the ground close to the water's edge. He returned to the buggy for the picnic supplies and the surprise he had for Ella.

"What's that?" Ella asked when she saw what he was holding.

He chuckled. "It's a fishing rod. Want to catch some fish later?" The water was so clear you could see fish swimming close to the surface. Simon and his father would fish here regularly to supplement the family's food supply. He hadn't realized a simple picnic down here by the stream would evoke so many wonderful memories. Today, they would make memories for Ella and Lillian to look back on. The thought warmed his heart.

As Lillian set out their lunch, Simon walked with Ella to the edge of the stream. "I can see the fishes!" she yelled in excitement.

"Shhh. You'll scare them away." He scooped the child up and let her watch as they swam back and forth in the water. The smile on her face was the only reward he needed.

"Food's ready." Lillian had pulled everything out of the basket and spread it across the blanket. It had been so long, he'd almost forgotten what a picnic was like. It had also been a very long time since he'd taken a day away from work, except for Sunday morning, when he attended church.

Not once had he thought about the repercussions on his family, but today would be a turning point. From today forward, he would spend as much time as possible with his wife and child. It wasn't as though he couldn't afford to put on more workers, because he could. And if that meant he got to spend additional time with his young family, so be it. Family was far more important to Simon than money. Thank goodness Tucker had reminded him of that. For someone who hadn't reached forty yet, his foreman sure was a smart fellow.

Ella sat on the blanket nibbling at her sandwich, one eye on the blueberry muffins. Lillian poured water for each of them. They ate quietly, enjoying the peacefulness of the area. At least Simon did. It seemed to lull his daughter to sleep as she rubbed her eyes, then lay down her head on her mama's lap. He watched as Lillian caressed the child's head until she was in a deep sleep. "Shhh," she said as he was about to speak. Of course, she was right. Ella was used to an afternoon nap, and today was no different than any other day. The pair ate while their daughter slept. Truth be told, Simon could easily lay down and nap himself.

He'd forgotten how serene it was out here. It had been some years since he'd ridden out this way, more's the pity. It was the kind of place you could come to clear your head, get your thoughts in order. Although that wasn't the purpose of today.

He reached out and covered Lillian's hand with his own. Her head shot up, and she studied him. She didn't say a word, but a shy smile formed on her face. He brought her hand to his lips and kissed it. Her hands were tiny compared to his, but then, she was quite short in stature – she didn't even reach as high as his shoulder. Perhaps that is the reason he felt so protective of her.

For the next thirty minutes or so, they sat quietly, eating their lunch and sipping on water. Ella continued to sleep as Simon drank in the fresh air and the sheer serenity of this place he'd loved so much as a young boy.

It wasn't long, and Ella was waking up and rubbing at her eyes. If she'd slept longer, it wouldn't have bothered him; he was enjoying simply being with his wife. He was beginning to understand Tucker's motivation, and silently thanked the man for making him understand why this was an important time for both he and Lillian.

"Shall we go for a short walk?" It meant he would get to hold his wife's hand a little longer, and anything that meant he got to touch her was fine with him. Simon was feeling a connection that wasn't there before. Oh sure, he'd enjoyed holding her, but this was different. He was seeing the real woman, the person, not just the mail order bride. He hadn't understood the difference before, but now it was becoming more clear to him.

Ella jumped up excitedly, now fully awake. A flock of birds, mostly sparrows and finches, suddenly flew skyward, having been disturbed by Ella's exuberance. The tranquility had been disturbed, but only momentarily. All would be back the way it should be in a matter of minutes, Simon knew.

They walked along the water's edge for what seemed a lifetime. "It's so peaceful here," Lillian told him. "Perhaps we can come back again some other time?"

"I'd like that," he said, regretting the fact they'd have to eventually leave. "Let's head back to our picnic spot now, so Ella can do some fishing." His wife nodded, and they headed back the way they came.

"I caught some fish!" Ella told Martha excitedly as she ran into the house.

Martha cast an eye over the mid-sized fish Ella held gingerly. "So you did. What a clever girl you are."

Simon had enjoyed the day far more than he ever anticipated and would have stayed far longer if the weather hadn't turned. The day was fairly warm when they started out, but had quite a chill in it by the time they left. This close to Christmas, it wouldn't be long and it would snow, and they'd need to rug up to go outside. Martha had the fire burning, which Simon appreciated, and was sure Lillian did too.

The smell of his wife's stew was enticing, and he already knew it would be tasty. "I might have time to make some biscuits to go with the stew," she suddenly said, heading toward the kitchen.

"Already done and in the oven," Martha said matter of factly. "As soon as they are out, I'll pop the pies in."

"You spoil us, Martha," Simon said, then pulled Lillian close against himself. "You too. I know you worked hard on that stew."

Simon knew he was an incredibly lucky man. He had a beautiful daughter, a housekeeper who looked after his home, and a wife by his side. Now all he needed was to have her love him the way he'd come to love her.

Simon awoke at dawn, just as he did every other day. He was taking today off as well, at Tucker's insistence. Both men knew the order would be fulfilled on time – it always was. It was the same every year; Simon stressed the order wouldn't be ready for the butcher in time, but they always had the cattle rounded up, with days to spare.

Still laying down, he watched as the sun rose. It was his favorite time of day. The beauty of it all was the pull, he was certain. Lillian stirred as he gently rolled over to face her. He hadn't meant to awaken her, but wanted to watch her as she slept. His wife was incredibly beautiful, and from the little he'd seen so far, was equally kind-hearted.

He knew so little about her, but still felt drawn to her. He thought he knew so much about her from the letters, but then… He mustn't rehash past indiscretions. Lillian wasn't her cousin, and she was the one he'd married. That was all that mattered now.

"Mama, Papa!" Ella came screeching into the bedroom and onto the bed, installing herself between them. He really needed to stop this terrible habit she had. The trouble was, he'd allowed it for most of her life. He couldn't stop it now because she might blame Lillian for the change, and that just wouldn't do.

"Ella," he said, trying not to upset her. "Please be more gentle. You gave Mama a terrible fright."

Their daughter immediately turned to Lillian. "I'm sorry, Mama. I didn't mean it." Tears shimmered in her eyes, and Lillian pulled Ella to her.

"It's fine, Ella, I'm fine. No need for tears." Her hands rubbed all over Ella's back, comforting the child. "But as Papa said, please be more gentle next time."

"Yes, Mama," she said as she hugged her new mother. It warmed his heart to see the two of them getting on so well. It was Simon's biggest fear of sending for a mail order bride. Now that he thought about it, once he'd mentioned Ella in his letters, Joy hadn't said a word about her. Hadn't asked any questions at all. He found it odd at the time, but didn't give it another thought. Now he knew he should have.

But had he done so, he wouldn't be married to Lillian; he would have married her cousin, who was clearly unsuitable. He definitely married the right cousin, and it gave him a warm feeling all over. His hope now was their union would produce heirs, but not because that's what he needed, but because it was what he wanted – to have children with his wonderful wife.

"Time to get up, I think," Lillian suddenly announced. It may have had something to do with the fact she was balancing on the edge of the bed. Ella did like to spread herself around.

She climbed out and pulled her robe around herself, sliding her feet into the warm slippers she'd brought with her.

"Can we go on a picnic again today, Papa?" Ella stared at him in anticipation, and he didn't have the heart to say no. Either way, he would spend the day with his two girls, getting to know them both. "Please Papa," she pleaded when he didn't respond.

Simon raised his eyebrows at his wife, trying to get her opinion. "Up to you," she said. "But perhaps not so long this time?"

"We're going on a picnic, we're going on a picnic," Ella chanted as she jumped up and down on the bed. And he didn't have the heart to say no.

He scooped his daughter up and placed her gently on the floor. "Why don't you go and get dressed?" he told her before Ella scooted away.

The moment she was out of the room, he climbed out of bed and stepped toward Lillian.

"You spoil her," she whispered, as Simon nibbled at her neck.

"I know," he said, leaning back to gaze into her face, then slowly moved toward her lips, and covered them with his own. Simon knew he'd found his soul-mate, and never wanted to let her go. He just hoped Lillian felt the same, but deep down inside, he didn't believe it was true. It broke his heart, as he wanted her to feel the happiness he had felt since she'd arrived.

Chapter Eight

"I, I don't know," Lillian said as she gingerly dipped her toes in the water. Simon took them to a different area this time. Still at the same stream, but in further along than the place they went to previously.

This area was more open, with fewer trees and more grass. The water was more shallow too, so they could sit on the edge and dangle their toes in the water.

"Go on Mama. It's not cold," Ella said as she giggled, her eyes wide with mischief. It was very obvious the water *was* cold, and her daughter was playing tricks on her.

"What about Papa? I don't see his feet in the water."

Simon pulled a face, then chuckled. The water was absolutely freezing, but she had no intention of telling him so. Besides, Ella was having a great time trying to trick them.

The water was so clear she could see the small white pebbles at the bottom of the stream. So clear, in fact, you could drink it, and she would happily do so. There were a few fish about, but none big enough to catch. Since the water was so shallow here, she figured they kept clear of this part of the stream.

"Do you visit here often?" She glanced across at Simon, who seemed to be deep in thought. He turned to face her, but seemed far away.

"Huh?"

"I asked if you visit here often? It's a lovely area, even better than where we were yesterday."

He moved closer to her and reached for her hand. "I used to come here as a young boy, when I wanted some time alone."

"I can see it would be a good place for that."

He suddenly stepped into the water with Ella and Lillian, pulling his wife to her feet. "I'm glad we've had some time together," he whispered. "I think we needed it."

She nodded, then rested her head on his chest. "We did." Lillian felt Ella's arms around her legs, trying to hug her, too. She leaned down and picked the child up, and the three of them stood there hugging each other for the longest time.

"I like having a mama," Ella said, and her heart thudded.

"I like having a family," Lillian said, her voice breaking. "This family in particular." She glanced from one to the other of them. "I love you both more than I ever imagined possible," she said, tears shimmering in her eyes.

Simon stared at her. "I love you too," he said, "But I dared not say it as I had no idea how you felt."

Ella pulled them both close to her little face. "I love you too," she said, and Lillian couldn't help the flood of tears that followed.

"What do you normally do for Christmas?" Lillian had contemplated the question for days, but hadn't broached it before.

Simon stared at her. "Well, all our workers are there, of course, and our neighbors are always invited."

She stared at him, open-mouthed. For a moment she thought he was joking, but his expression was so serious, there was no way he was joking. Martha worked in the kitchen as the husband and wife sat sipping coffee. Time ticked on and not a word passed between them, but Lillian's heart pounded.

How would she cope, especially once Martha was gone? She'd promised to stay until Christmas Eve, but no longer.

"For goodness' sakes," Martha said, throwing a kitchen cloth on the countertop. "Tell the truth and don't scare the poor woman away!"

Simon suddenly dissolved into laughter, and Lillian was ready to throttle him. "You're joking?" She put her hand to her heart. "Don't ever do that again. You scared ten years off my life."

She put her coffee on the side table, and he pulled his wife toward him, settling her into his lap. "I wouldn't do that to you," he said, his eyes gazing into hers. "Martha has everything under control, so don't worry your pretty little head over it."

She studied him. Simon was a very handsome man, but she still couldn't always read him. He did like to joke, but he was also very serious at times. He seemed a lot like her in many ways – when he loved; he loved deeply. It was very easy to see he adored his daughter, and he had told her he loved her. Not just at the stream, but several times since.

Lillian didn't know what she would ever do without this wonderful family she'd stumbled onto. If it hadn't been for her cousin's selfishness, she wouldn't be here now. Something she would be forever grateful for.

The quiet was suddenly broken by the men piling into the house. She hadn't realized how late it was. She pulled out of Simon's lap, but he held her tight against him. "Where are you going?" he whispered.

"The men…"

"Have surely seen husband and wife snuggling before. If not, their loss." His breath was warm against her cheek, and suddenly Lillian wanted nothing more than to kiss him. As if he could read her mind, he kissed her cheek, then turned her head to have access to her lips. He kissed her long and deeply, leaving Lillian breathless.

She wanted nothing more than to be alone with her wonderful husband, a man she didn't know until recently. Fate moved in mysterious ways, and she was more than a little pleased about the outcome of this particular adventure.

Epilogue

Two years later…

"Mama! Papa!" Ella's squeal had Simon running. "It's snowing!"

Simon stood behind his daughter and watched mesmerized as snow fell in the yard. It was by no means heavy, but was still evident on the grass, with small patches of snow showing through.

"Can we build a snowman?" She turned to look at him, her little eyes opened wide in anticipation.

He hated to say it, but she had to understand. "There's not enough snow to build a snowman yet. Perhaps in a few days, or a week." He picked Ella up and tapped her nose with his finger. "Be patient, little one." She screwed up her face, which made Simon chuckle.

"Mama," Ella said as Lillian entered the room. "Look at all the snow!" Simon watched with delight the expression on his daughter's face when his wife entered the room. It was as though she hadn't seen her mother for months. Her little arms reached out to Lillian, wanting to be held by her.

"We've talked about this before, haven't we, Ella?" Simon's voice was firm, but still held compassion.

Her little head bent, she pouted as Ella always did when she was trying to wrap her father around her little finger. "But I want Mama to hold me. I love her hugs."

"You're a big girl now, and far too heavy for Mama. Why, you're nearly six!"

Ella's head shot up, and she glared at him. "I'm nearly seven," she said with conviction. "I'm not a baby anymore."

She stared at him until he couldn't take it anymore and laughed. "I know. I was trying to trick you." When he glanced her way, Lillian was trying to force back a smile. "How about I hold you while you hug Mama?"

"Or better still, Mama could sit down and give you a big hug."

Lillian sounded tired, and Simon immediately put Ella to the floor and studied his wife. "Let me help you," he answered quietly, putting an arm about her shoulders and guiding her to the nearest chair. "Should I call the doc?"

"I'm simply tired, I'm not in labor."

He snatched up a blanket, draping it over her very swollen belly and her legs, then put another log on the fire next to her, ensuring Lillian didn't get a chill.

"It's almost time for Samson to be fed."

Pride ran through Simon at the thought of his son. His first born with Lillian. She wanted to name him after Simon's father, and he couldn't be happier. Samson Simon Watson. Good strong family names; names he hoped would be passed down from generation to generation.

As if on cue, Samson cried. Lillian began to stand, but he insisted she stay right where she was. She was so close to giving birth, and he didn't want her to exert herself, but save her energy for the birth.

Simon stared down into the angelic face of his son as he changed his saturated diaper. His life had changed for the better the day Lillian had arrived, and he couldn't ask for a more perfect life or family. They'd had their problems at the start, but love always finds a way. With God on their side, it had to work out, and he had put his trust in the Lord to help them through the rough patches, and He did.

With the diaper changed, and the baby now dry and tightly wrapped as Lillian had taught him, he carried Samson to his mother. Ella came running over from the window where she'd continued to watch the snow falling. She leaned in and kissed her baby brother who was already crawling.

"It's almost Christmas," she told Samson. "You'll love Christmas when you are a bit bigger." Simon could barely hold back his grin. Ella was a perfect big sister, and soon she would have another sibling to love as well. He silently prayed his thanks for his wonderful family; the family he never dreamed he would ever have.

The End

From the Author

Thank you so much for reading my book – I hope you enjoyed it.

I would greatly appreciate you leaving a review where you purchased, even if it is only a one-liner. It helps to have my books more visible!

About the Author

Multi-published, award-winning and bestselling author Cheryl Wright, former secretary, debt collector, account manager, writing coach, and shopping tour hostess, loves reading.

She writes both historical and contemporary western romance, as well as romantic suspense.

She lives in Melbourne, Australia, and is married with two adult children and has six grandchildren. When she's not writing, she can be found in her craft room making greeting cards.

Links:

Website: *http://www.cheryl-wright.com/*

Blog: *http://romance-authors.com/*

Facebook Reader Group:
https://www.facebook.com/groups/cherylwrightauthor/

Join My Newsletter:

https://cheryl-wright.com/newsletter/

www.ingramcontent.com/pod-product-compliance
Lightning Source LLC
Chambersburg PA
CBHW070631120726
47909CB00004B/1391

* 9 780645 250862 *